I Dance in My Red Pajamas

Edith Thacher Hurd

I Dance in My Red Pajamas

Pictures by

Emily Arnold McCully

Harper & Row, Publishers

I Dance in My Red Pajamas
 Printed in the United States of America. For information address Harper & Row, Publishers, Inc., 10 East 53rd Street, New York, N.Y. 10022.

Library of Congress Cataloging in Publication Data
Hurd, Edith Thacher, date
I dance in my red pajamas.

Summary: A young girl visits with her grandparents who feel the best day is a noisy day.
I. McCully, Emily Arnold, ill. II. Title.
PZ7.H9561ad 1982 [E] 81-47721
ISBN 0-06-022699-4 AACR2
ISBN 0-06-022700-1 (lib. bdg.)

"Don't be too noisy, little Jenny,"
Mother says.
"Don't jump around and shout
when you go to visit your
Granny and your Grandpa,"
Father says.

I only smile and say,
"Of course not,"
because my mother and my father
do not know what my
Granny and my Grandpa and I do
when I go to visit them.

My mother and my father think
my Granny and my Grandpa are very old.
They don't seem old to me,
except my Granny's hair is white,
and my Grandpa's just a little deaf,
so he sometimes shouts at me.

When I go to their house,
I take my red pajamas.
I take my toothbrush.
And I take my Lion too.

I ring the bell,
and when he sees me,
Grandpa shouts,
"Hey Granny, look who's here."

I shout right back,
"It's me, Jenny.
I've come to spend the night."

My Granny hugs me.
My Grandpa's tall.
He looks down and smiles at me.

When I go inside the house,
I look around.
I like the way
it's always just the same.
It smells of things that Granny's cooking:
chicken, and blueberry pie.
There are flowers:
wild roses and daisies.

Grandpa takes me by the hands.
"Let's play the whirling game,"
he shouts.
I go whirling, whirling, whirling,
And I'm singing, singing, singing.
"Oh, I'm busy, busy, busy,
getting dizzy, dizzy, dizzy."

When Grandpa puts me down,
I wobble and I topple
and I sing my whirling song,
"Oh, I'm busy, busy, busy,
getting dizzy, dizzy, dizzy,"
until I fall into Granny's lap.

"Come on, Jenny," Grandpa says.
"I'm going to build a house outside,
for Catarina."
Catarina is Granny's big, fat, yellow cat.
"Nonsense," Granny says.
"Why can't Catarina live in our house,
the way she always has?"

"Because she wants to come in
when she is out," grumbles Grandpa.
"Then she wants to go out
when she is in. Cats are like that."
"Nonsense," Granny says again.
"Catarina will never live
in a house by herself.
Build a house for a mouse instead."
Grandpa and I laugh,
but we don't pay any attention.

Grandpa gets his hammer,
and I get mine.
We bang and we bang and we bang.

But Granny is right.
Catarina just yawns
when we try to put her into the house
that we built for her.

I help Granny fix supper.
I help her roll out the crust
and whip the cream
for the blueberry pie.

I put knives and forks and spoons
on the big kitchen table.
Grandpa and I smack our lips
and laugh at each other when we have finished,
because we are all blue,
from the blueberry pie.

When we have washed the dishes,
Granny runs the water
in the old-fashioned bathtub.
It is big enough to swim in.
It has feet like four claws underneath it.

Boats sail with me.
Fish and ducks swim
around and around me.
Soap bubbles cover me.

I splash like the waves
at the beach in the summer.
I make fountains like a whale
swimming under the water.

Grandpa shouts from downstairs,
"Stop sloshing the water, Jenny.
It's dripping down on my head."
I stop slopping about
because Grandpa doesn't have any
hair on the top of his head.

I put on my red pajamas.
I brush my teeth.

I help Grandpa bring in big logs
for the fire.
"Why don't cats like to live in houses
all by themselves?" I ask Grandpa.
"Perhaps they get lonely," he answers.
Then I tell Grandpa,
"I think cats and dogs
like to live in houses with people.
They like it best to be in houses
where we are."
"So do I," Grandpa says slowly.

I sit on the floor,
with my Lion on one side
and Catarina on the other.
We watch the fire spurting and spitting.
We listen to the pops and the crackles.
Granny begins to play the piano
very softly.
And I dance in my red pajamas.

When she plays louder,
Grandpa and I dance.
We clap and we stomp
as loud as we can.

Granny calls,
"Swing your partner
and away you go.
Swing your partner
and a do-si-do."

Then Granny and Grandpa dance.
They dance without any music,
just humming the tune to each other.
When they are through,
Grandpa says,
"That's the way Granny and I used
to dance on soft summer nights
long ago."

I had never thought about Granny
and Grandpa dancing together.
But I am too sleepy to say anything more.
So Grandpa picks me up, piggyback
and takes me upstairs.
Catarina is already there.

Granny tucks me into my bed.
We give each other hugs
and Lion too.
"Good night, Granny," I say.
"Good night, Jenny," she says.

But Grandpa says,
"Oh, what a beautiful, lovely, noisy day."